One in a Million

WINTERVALE PROMISES: BOOK 13

MELODIE MARCH

Pine St. Publishing

Harmony Sutton sliced yet another small square of cake in half and popped it into her mouth. She relished the delicious flavors of kumquat and chocolate. The combination of sweet and tart citrus mixed with dark chocolate reminded her of Christmas, which was perfect. She and Sebastian were getting married on December 17th with a holiday theme.

"Try this one, honey. It's perfect."

Sebastian accepted the forkful of cake even though he already knew how it tasted. The restaurant he managed, Wren & Candle, was catering their wedding and his boss Juniper made all the cake samples. Her chocolate kumquat cheesecake was a colossal hit during the holidays and she promised to recreate it as a wedding cake option.

"That's my favorite, for sure. But we'll have to have some cupcakes on the side for people who don't do chocolate. I'm sure Juniper won't mind. Or maybe we can get Belle to make some?"

The whole Sutton family was sitting at the dining room table with them, tasting cakes and discussing the menu. The only one missing was Harmony's sister, Amber, who had to work late at the hospital. Her brothers, Charlie Jr. and Carver, were stuffing cake in their mouths faster than Sebastian and Harmony could taste it. Harmony reached across the table and smacked their hands.

"When you get married, you can taste all the cake you want. But leave me something to choose from!"

CJ waved her hand away.

"You know you're going to pick that chocolate orange one. And I didn't have time to eat after class. Let me snack, woman!"

Their mother, Tara, yanked the tray out of her sons' reach.

"Yeah, and you're going to load up on sugar at the festival, so cool it. The two of you act like you're kids again on Halloween. I'm not even sure I should let you go alone."

Harmony laughed so hard she snorted as the boys whined in unison.

"Mooooom."

Sebastian was used to the bickering, since he'd been a part of their family from long before he and Harmony got engaged. But he still couldn't help but laugh when they all got together and started acting like kids again. It made planning the wedding a blast, though it was also taking them twice as long to get anything finished. Thank goodness they still had a month.

Tara stood up from the table and started ushering them all into the hallway.

"Alright, kids. Hurry up and go to the festival before you miss the haunted City Hall thing! I have work to do and I don't want you here when the sugar high kicks in."

They all gathered up their coats and, as Harmony was looking for her purse, a cell phone rang.

Carver felt his pockets.

"Not mine."

Sebastian and Harmony shook their heads. CJ finally dug his vibrating phone out of his work bag and looked at the caller ID in confusion. It wasn't a number he recognized.

"Maybe it's Amber calling from the hospital." Charlie put the phone on speaker. "Can you make it to the festival after all, slacker?"

"Excuse me?"

Everyone jumped when they heard the voice of an unexpected stranger.

"I'm sorry. I thought you were my sister. Who is this?"

The woman cleared her throat, as if she was nervous.

"Mr. Charles Sutton Jr.?"

"Yes..."

"This is Mina Barkley from International Transplant Coordination Services. Several years ago, you took part in a blood drive and signed a consent form to be contacted should you be a donor match for a person in need of bone marrow or an organ."

Charlie gulped and everyone in the room turned and stared at him with their eyes wide in confusion.

"I... yes, I sort of remember. Why are you calling me?"

The entire family could see the panic on his face as he waited for the woman to get to her point.

"Mr. Sutton, I won't dance around the issue. There is a young woman in Cornwall, in the United Kingdom, who has been searching for a kidney donor for some time as she has a very rare blood type. You share that blood type, Mr. Sutton. I was wondering if you'd be willing to further discuss this matter with me next week? I'm in Raleigh, North Carolina, but can fly to Vermont before Thanksgiving."

Charlie was frozen where he stood, and it didn't seem like he could say a word.

"Mr. Sutton? Are you willing to speak to me in person?"

As he stared at the shocked faces of his family, he didn't know what to say...

Was he willing to talk to this woman about giving a kidney to someone he'd never met? Was he willing to take a chance like this on a complete stranger?

Chapter One

MARIN - CORNWALL, ENGLAND

"Emily! Emily, love, I left my medication in the kitchen! Can you bring it to me?"

Marin Walker was about to start a live stream for the travel site she wrote for, *The Budget Wayfarer*. When she graduated college, the website's editor hired her to cover vacation options in her beloved hometown of Cornwall. It was the perfect job; she could work from the home she shared with her best friend, Emily Marsh, and it was flexible for dealing with her Alport Syndrome. The genetic kidney condition made it difficult for her to work on someone else's schedule, but writing proved to be a welcome respite from everything else going on in her life.

She also *loved* talking about Cornwall.

"Here babe," Emily said as she bounded into Marin's sunny office. She was still in a bathrobe from her morning shower and she piled her bright red curls up in a bun on top of her head. "You can't forget to take these. You're supposed to take them as soon as you get up."

She squeezed her friend's hand as she took the bottle from her. Ever since Marin's mom passed away when they were seventeen, Emily made it her mission to be Marin's caretaker. She didn't even

5

let her fiancé hover as much as Emily... not that Ashton showed much interest in caretaking. He had a trust fund to deplete, and that was his primary focus.

"I'm sorry. I was so distracted getting prepared for this live stream. We're talking about The Eden Project today and you know how much I love my biomes."

Emily laughed and kissed Marin on the top of the head.

"Don't go on too long about the partridges."

She skipped out of the office to get ready for her job at the cafe around the corner from their small cottage by the sea. Marin was fifteen minutes from starting her live stream when her cell rang. It was Ashton. He was in Majorca on holiday with his family for the third time that year. He invited Marin to come with them, but the last time they traveled together, his mother Anne bought first class plane tickets for everyone... except Marin. Her reasoning was that, "the sick girl doesn't know any better, anyway. No need to waste a perfectly good first-class ticket on a coach girl."

Marin didn't care much for Anne Cunningham, but she'd tolerated her since she and Ashton started dating as kids.

"Hello, love," Marin said when she answered the phone and put it on speaker. "I can hear sunshine. Are you having a lovely time?"

Ashton scoffed.

"Hardly. Mother booked me into a junior suite. It's positively unsuitable. You'd like it, though."

Marin rolled her eyes. "I don't have a lot of time to talk, Ash. I'm about to start a live stream for the site. Can you call me tonight?"

"We have reservations at the restaurant in the hotel. Mother knows the chef, so we'll probably be there all night. Why can't you talk now?"

He was whining, which he did when he was in his mother's company for too long. It was like he regressed twenty years and became a petulant child again.

"Ashton, I can't just skip out on my job to talk because you're not busy. Over twelve-thousand people signed up for this."

He sighed the way he always did when she talked about her job. Ashton didn't think writing for a travel website was a *proper* job, which was ironic, as he didn't have a job at all. He would just show up at his father's law office in London twice a month, sleep at an empty desk on the partner's floor, and collect a massive paycheck for doing nothing.

Ashton didn't even go to law school. Marin still hadn't figured out how his father was justifying the payment.

She looked at the time on her computer and her stomach flip-flopped. She was a few minutes from starting.

"I have to go, love. I'm sorry. Call me whenever you can, okay?"

"Wait, Marin! I'm bored! I want to…"

She didn't give him a chance to finish and disconnected, so he couldn't continue arguing. If she didn't hang up then, he would keep her on long past the start time for the stream. Before she went live, she ruffled her wavy hair one last time, spritzed on some rosewater mist that made her skin look dewy, and took her medication before she forgot again. Marin took a big breath and adjusted her hearing aids, then went to hit connect. Except, just as she did, her phone rang again.

"Come on, Ashton. You're in paradise. Go swimming!"

She picked up her phone to ignore the call, but it wasn't her fiancé. It was a number she didn't recognize from the US. Curiosity got the better of her and she answered.

"This is Marin?"

A cheerful woman with a southern American accent answered her.

"Hello, Miss Walker! This is Mina Barkley from International Transplant Coordination Services. Marin, honey… How quickly can you get on a plane to Vermont in the United States?"

She was so startled she almost dropped the phone in her lap.

"How quickly can I... what? I don't understand. Why would I go to Vermont?"

There was a slight pause, but when Mina answered, Marin could practically hear her smiling.

"We found you a kidney, honey. We finally found you the gift you've been waiting for all these years."

Marin stared at her computer blankly, unable to believe what she'd just heard. A message popped up on the screen from her boss at *The Budget Wayfarer*.

Marcus Swift: *Marin, where are you? Everyone is waiting!*

"Miss Walker? Are you there? Oh, shoot. I hope I didn't lose my connection."

"No! No, I'm here. I just... I can't believe it. This is real?"

"It's real," Mina said. "I'm emailing you the details right now. Your donor is in Wintervale, Vermont. The transplant will take place at the UVM Medical Center in Burlington and your donor's family has offered to host you while you recuperate in the States. I just need you to let me know when you can leave Cornwall and we will book you a ticket!"

This time, Marin *did* drop her phone, and she immediately started crying. Before she knew what was happening, Emily was at her side, half her makeup done and still in a towel.

"Marin? What's wrong? What's going on?"

She threw her arms around her best friend.

"I'm going to America, Emily! I'm going to get a kidney!"

That was all Emily needed to hear to cry, too. After years of waiting, it was finally happening...

The only thing between Marin and a new life was a flight to Vermont.

"Wintervale, here I come!" she said as she wiped away tears.

Charlie Sutton Jr. sat behind his desk scrolling through a website about Alport Syndrome while his second period calculus students took an exam. It was his last day of teaching for the school year at Wintervale High. Soon, Marin would land at the airport in Burlington and they would start the transplant process.

He was trying to keep busy, to distract himself from his nerves, but he found his thoughts drifting to the English girl, who would soon wing her way to the US. Not long ago, CJ knew nothing about the rare genetic disorder.

Now, his house was full of pages he'd printed off the internet as he tried to educate himself about Marin's condition.

He was so engrossed in trying to teach himself how to introduce himself in British Sign Language that he didn't notice all of his students stopped writing. It took a few minutes for him to register the distinct lack of the sound of pencils scribbling on paper. CJ looked up from his computer to see a classroom full of kids all staring at him, smiling.

It was creepy.

"What's going on? There's no way you all finished at the same time. I don't want to have the 'open book and sharing notes aren't the same thing' conversation again."

His most advanced student, Mattie Slater, got up from her desk and walked up to him with a card in her hand. She was grinning as she handed it to him and bouncing up and down on her toes.

"We all chipped in and got you a present, Mr. Sutton."

CJ was notorious at Wintervale High for being a giant softie in the body of a linebacker, but it took effort to fight back tears in front of his students.

"Aw, come on. You shouldn't have done that. You need to save your money for college, or your gap years, or whatever."

The kids chuckled, as one boy in the back yelled, "Open it, Mr. Sutton!"

CJ untucked the envelope flap and pulled out the card. It had two little smiling cartoon kidneys on the outside. Inside, in bright pink bubble letters, it said, ***"Thanks for sharing your spare!"*** Behind the card, CJ found a gift certificate for three dinner deliveries from Wren & Candle, the restaurant that was literally across the meadow from his house. His place belonged to Juniper Thatcher, who also owned Wren & Candle. CJ couldn't help but laugh.

"This is an amazing gift, everyone. Thank you! You really didn't have to, but I appreciate it."

Mattie gave him a gentle punch on the shoulder.

"You didn't have to help this girl, but you are. The least we could do is buy you dinner while you're recuperating."

Reece Thornton, who was graduating in June, leaned over sideways in his seat.

"Are you going to bring her to school to meet us, Mr. S? We don't get a lot of Irish girls in Wintervale!"

CJ shook his head. "You're still not, Reece. She's from Cornwall. Cornwall is closer to France than it is to Ireland. Maybe you should have taken that European History elective and learned some geography this semester instead of two study halls."

A chorus of "oohs" filled the room as Reece's cheeks turned red. CJ waved at them to settle down.

"I'm kidding. I'm kidding, Reece. We'll see how things go once she gets here. But just in case, I want you to keep practicing your BSL so she feels welcome. Okay, no more sappy stuff. You have twenty minutes to finish that exam and don't think I'm going to go easy on you because you almost made me cry! Back to work, young minds."

Mattie hustled back to her seat and the sound of pencils clicking against paper on hardwood desks filled the room once again. CJ sighed as he turned back to his laptop and scanned through a list of common BSL words. The transplant coordinator said Marin could hear pretty well with her hearing aids in, but he still wanted to show her he was putting in effort.

Lord knew his family was *more* than prepared for her arrival in a few days...

He just hoped a car full of Suttons wouldn't overwhelm her on her first day in the States. Five of them, plus his sister Harmony's husband Sebastian, were going to the airport in Burlington to meet Marin when her plane landed. Even *CJ* found it overwhelming to walk through his mom's front door and get swarmed by his family.

He had his fingers crossed Marin was ready for the Sutton-based chaos awaiting her in Wintervale.

Chapter Three

MARIN

Marin was exhausted as she walked to the baggage claim at Burlington International Airport, but she was intent on meeting her host family on her own two feet. She left the airport in Newquay at one in the afternoon, then flew from Dublin to New York, and New York to Burlington.

Even after over ten hours flying, and five-and-a-half hours of layovers, it was only midnight on the East Coast of the US. Marin was practically dead on her feet. All she wanted to do was sleep for three days, but she knew the best thing to do was to hit the ground running and adjust to the new time zone as soon as possible.

Thank goodness it was midnight; that gave her the perfect excuse to go right to bed.

Because it was late, the airport was relatively quiet. Which is why it was so startling when Marin reached her baggage carousel and saw a massive family waving at her and shouting, holding up a sign that read, **Welcome to Vermont, Marin!** She was so shocked; she screamed and dropped her carry-on bag. For a moment, she hesitated, which was all it took for most of the family to charge her and wrap her up in a massive group hug. Two of the guys stayed back and one of them covered his face in embarrassment, which made Marin laugh.

The older woman finally let go of her and reached out to brush some of Marin's hair away from her face.

"Oh, sweetie, it's so good to have you here! I'm Tara Sutton and these are my kids… and my kid-in-law."

She pointed to a cute guy in a short-sleeved flannel shirt who waved at Marin with a shy smile. He put his arm around the woman next to him, who was practically glowing as she nuzzled into him. Tara rolled her eyes.

"Newlyweds."

Mina, the transplant coordinator, already filled Marin in on the whole Sutton family. Still, she wanted to be polite and let them introduce themselves, especially because Tara seemed so proud of her family.

"It's so nice to meet all of you," Marin said as she tried to pick up her bag again. She barely got it off the floor before one son, who was wearing a Hawaiian shirt, jeans, and covered in tattoos, rushed over and took it out of her hands.

"Marin, this is my second oldest, Carver, holding your bag. This girl in the pink PJs and fuzzy slippers is my baby, Amber. She's a nurse, and she's going to be taking care of you while you're here. The lovebirds are my daughter Harmony and her husband, Sebastian. And back there, looking as mortified by us as ever, is Charlie Junior. You already know him as CJ."

He looked nothing like Marin imagined him. CJ was at least 6'5, with broad shoulders and hugely muscled arms. He had a perfectly groomed beard and huge, piercing brown eyes. As soon as she saw CJ, she was overwhelmed by the urge to cry as the enormity of what he was doing for her hit her for the first time. This complete stranger was giving up a part of himself so she could live. Without even thinking, she charged through the rest of the family and threw her arms around him.

At first, CJ seemed a little taken aback. After a moment, though, he chuckled softly and wrapped his arms around her.

"Hey, don't get weepy, now. You're probably dehydrated after all that time on airplanes."

Marin stepped away and wiped the tears from her cheeks.

"I am, actually. Is there anywhere we can get something to eat? Airplane food doesn't really agree with me."

The whole family laughed and shook their heads. Amber took Marin's hand and swung it like they were already best friends.

"It's a two-hour drive back to Wintervale and *nothing* is open after ten. But one thing you don't have to worry about in the Sutton house is food. Let's get your bags and get out of here. You must be ready to settle down."

As Amber held on to her and the guys went to the luggage carousel to retrieve her two massive suitcases, Marin realized that for the first time in a long time, she felt like she was part of a family...

And she'd only been in Vermont for half an hour.

MARIN SLEPT the whole ride from Burlington back to Wintervale. She tried her best to stay awake and, under normal circumstances, it would have been easy. The Suttons took two cars to pick her up, so she got in the back of an SUV with Tara, Amber, and CJ. Once they were on the highway, she couldn't keep her eyes open. Despite the family's cheerful chatter, she fell asleep on Amber's shoulder and missed the entire ride. It wasn't until she felt the rumble of a stone driveway under the tires that she opened her eyes and sat up.

"Oh my goodness, has it been two hours already?"

Amber smiled as she adjusted her arm, causing a little *crack* to echo through the car. "It sure has, babe. I think you may have drooled on me a little."

Marin was humiliated.

"I'm so sorry! It was such a long flight and..."

CJ smacked his sister's leg from the front seat.

"Ignore her. She's just messing with you. We'll get you something to eat when you get inside and then you can head to bed."

Marin tried not to laugh as Amber hit CJ back and they bickered until Tara whistled at them, which made them both shut up immediately. She parked the car in front of a brightly lit colonial home straight out of Marin's favorite movie, *Little Women*. From the double chimneys, to the gray clapboard and the welcoming bright red door, it looked too perfect to be real.

"Oh, Mrs. Sutton! Your home is beautiful!"

They got out of the car just as Sebastian pulled up behind them with Harmony and Carver. The boys retrieved all of Marin's bags as Tara unlocked the door.

"Please, call me Tara. Thank you, sweetie. It's been in our family for generations. I'm just happy I have space for all my babies, even if they come and go like boarders."

Everyone but Amber groaned as they walked inside. The house was even more beautiful once Marin stepped across the threshold. The walls were painted in bright, classic colors or covered in gorgeous patterned wallpaper. Every room contained a combination of antiques and homey furniture, perfect for a big family. She may have missed her little cottage by the sea, but Marin could easily imagine living in the Suttons' wonderful house forever.

Tara ushered her behind Sebastian, Carver, and CJ, who were making a beeline for a door off the living room.

"You're going to be staying in the bedroom down here, Marin," Tara said as she opened the door. "We figured it would be easier for you after the surgery, plus it has its own private bathroom."

She flipped on the light, and Marin gasped. The bedroom was bigger than hers and Emily's combined. They painted it a beautiful shade of sand with ocean blue accents, had a plush carpet on the floor, tons of comfy furniture, and the biggest bed Marin had ever seen in her life. There was even a little sitting area near a massive television that could also be seen from the bed.

"Mrs... Tara, this is too much. I must be putting someone out of their room."

Tara scowled over at Carver, who leaned against the wall and shook his head.

"This *was* my room," Carver said. "But I moved to Hadleigh to live with a friend from the shop. It's all yours, Marin."

She felt tears welling up again, but she saw CJ wink at her and quickly sniffed them away.

"Thank you. All of you. Truly. I can't even begin to tell you..."

Harmony sidled up to her and gave her a tight, comforting hug.

"Marin, you can't spend the next two months here thanking us all the time. Let's just call that the last 'thank you' of your visit and instead, you focus on relaxing and healing."

Marin stifled the urge to thank Harmony and nodded instead. Tara walked to the door and started shoving her kids out.

"Is there anyone you need to call to let them know you got here?"

"I texted my best friend when the plane landed, but then my phone died. I'll call my fiancé tomorrow. He won't be awake now, anyway."

Tara looked at her watch. "Isn't it 7:30 in the UK? He doesn't have a job?"

Marin sighed. "Not this month. This month he's vacationing in Spain and sleeping until noon."

"Uh-huh," Tara said, her eyebrow raised suspiciously. "Well, plug that phone in, sweetie. I picked you up some adapters. Then put on something comfy and join us in the kitchen for a snack. After that, we'll all head to bed."

Tara closed the door behind her and as soon as she was alone,

Marin collapsed onto the giant bed with a contented sigh. It wouldn't be an easy two months, but if she was spending them in a place like this?

She could get used to it.

Chapter Four

CJ

Tara was emptying the fridge of everything she made earlier in the day to prepare for Marin's arrival. There were sandwich platters, bowls of potato and pasta salad, sliced fruit, and a tray of cupcakes from the bakery downtown. She also took out two pitchers of tea, a bucket of ice, and several bottles of sparkling water. Amber walked up behind her and stole a piece of pineapple from the fruit.

"Jeez, mom. It's a midnight snack, not a 4th of July picnic for the whole town."

Her mother scowled at her. "The transplant coordinator said she had specific dietary restrictions that they probably wouldn't be able to accommodate at the airport. Everything has to be low in potassium and salt. So, anything with her name on it, just stay away."

Carver picked up the bowl of potato salad and shook it around.

"There isn't any salt in the food? Is it going to be like this for the entire two months?"

CJ snatched the bowl from his brother's hand and smacked him on the back of the head. "You'll live. God forbid you make your own food for a change. Besides, you don't need that much salt. It's bad for your heart."

Tara took the potato salad from CJ and put it back on the counter.

"Charlie, don't hit your brother. But he's right, Carver. You aren't a teenager anymore. You need to watch what you eat."

CJ couldn't help but laugh. This was what it was like every time he came home. He and his siblings all turned into kids again; a part of him really missed it. Amber was the only one still living at home because she was saving money to buy her own place. Sebastian and Harmony lived in grandmother's old place close to downtown, and Carver was in Hadleigh now. Tara didn't admit it often, but she really missed having all her kids under the same roof.

He could see it whenever they came back. She was always happiest when she was fussing over her children, especially now that she was only working part-time at Hadleigh Hope Hospital. When the transplant coordinator asked if Tara would let Marin live with her while she recuperated from the surgery, his mom jumped at the chance. It meant she had someone else under her roof to worry about again.

"CJ," Tara said, startling him from his daydreaming. "Did Mina say anything to you about Marin being engaged?"

"Huh? Oh, no. I noticed the ring, though. Why?"

She scrunched up her forehead like the potato salad went bad.

"I don't know. I don't like the sound of him. He doesn't sound good enough for her."

Harmony laughed as she rolled up a slice of cheese and nibbled it.

"Mom, you just met her! You don't even know her fiancé. How could you possibly know anything about her relationship?"

Tara tapped her finger to her nose.

"You know I have a sense for these things. Something is off there."

CJ gestured at her to zip it because he heard the door to

Marin's room open. When she walked into the kitchen, she was wearing red flannel pajamas and a pair of soft, furry boots. She piled her long hair up on top of her head in a loose bun and, for the first time since she arrived, he noticed her hearing aids. That was when he realized he forgot his entire plan, so he quickly said "hello" and "welcome to Vermont" to her in BSL.

Marin smiled and clapped her hands together.

"That was so sweet of you, CJ! I can't even remember the last time I signed with anyone."

"Oh," he said, afraid he had insulted her. "Mina said you were hard of hearing and I thought..."

"No, it was lovely! I used to sign with my mother all the time. But I got these hearing aids a few years ago and they've really helped. Now, I only sign with my roommate from time to time. And you learned BSL! It was truly thoughtful."

CJ felt a bit sheepish for a moment, but Amber was quick to pick up on it.

"I actually learned ASL when I started at the hospital and it's been really helpful. You'll have to show me some differences while you're here."

Marin, Amber, and Tara started chatting about their work at the hospital, which gave CJ a reprieve to join his brother and sister at the table. Sebastian was in the other room dealing with a late night delivery issue at Wren & Candle, where he was the manager.

"She's pretty cute, Charlie," Harmony said as she gave her brother a gentle punch on the chest. "Maybe you two can hang out together while you're healing."

"Dude, mom *literally* just said Marin has a fiancé. Besides, I won't hit on the girl I'm giving my kidney to. She'll think I miss it and am just trying to keep it close by."

Carver laughed so hard, he snorted, which caused everyone to turn and stare. Harmony tried to match her brother's laughter, but it seemed forced.

"Sorry for interrupting! Sibling stuff."

CJ rolled his eyes and dropped his head in hands. "You two are the worst."

Sebastian walked up and kissed Harmony on the head.

"I'm sorry, honey. There was an issue with the produce delivery. Harley was going to meet the truck, but he got stuck at the Hadleigh location. Juniper is out of town with Enid. It's a mess. I'll drop you off at home and head over there."

As always, Tara seemed to sense the impending departure of one of her children and started making plates for them to take home with them. Carver would inevitably be right behind them, so she turned her intent gaze on CJ.

"Charlie, you're staying over tonight, right? This way, you can show Marin around when she gets up tomorrow?"

There was no way he was getting out of it now. He kept a bag in his car, anyway, because this happened at least once a week.

"Sure, I'll just stay in my old room."

Tara smiled triumphantly as she poured Marin a glass of water. "Alright, young lady. While you're in my house, I'm going to treat you like one of my babies, and that means it's time for bed. You sleep as late as you want tomorrow. We can worry about getting you on our time Sunday morning."

CJ walked his brother, sister, and brother-in-law outside. Before Harmony got in the car, she gave CJ a hug and whispered to him.

"That girl is special, Charlie. Don't be stubborn."

Then she pinched his arm and jumped in the car before he could reciprocate. He loved his sister, but she was an even better meddler than their mother. Marin was only in Wintervale for two months, then she had a life to go back to on the other side of the ocean...

In the meantime, he was looking forward to getting to know her. Even if it *was* only for a little while.

Chapter Five

MARIN

When Marin woke up the next morning, the warm sunshine was pouring through the windows and across the bed. She stretched her arms out and then rolled across the pillows, nuzzling up to them. Everything was so soft and plush; she felt like she was sleeping on a cloud. If it wasn't such a beautiful day, she might have stayed in that bed until lunch. It was already after ten, though, and she could hear the Suttons chatting in the kitchen. She put on her robe, quickly went through her morning routine, then rushed out to join everyone. The sight she saw made her heart swell.

When she was growing up, it was usually just Marin and her mom in their cottage by the sea. Emily spent a lot of time with them since they had been inseparable most of their lives, but mornings were always just for Marin and her mom. So, when she walked into the Suttons' dining room and saw the breakfast table packed with people, she couldn't help but laugh. Harmony and Sebastian were both there, as was CJ, who stayed the night. Amber was pouring herself a cup of coffee at the counter as Tara finished a stack of pancakes at the stove.

"Good morning, Sunshine!" Tara said as she handed the plate to Amber to carry to the table. "How did you sleep?"

"Like the dead!"

Everyone at the table looked at each other awkwardly for a moment, like they weren't sure if it was appropriate to laugh or not. CJ was the first one to chuckle.

"You're dark. I like that."

The mood in the room softened, and she sat in the chair between CJ and Harmony. As soon as she scooted up to the table, the whole family started loading her plate with way more food than she could eat. Most mornings, she had oatmeal or some fruit. She couldn't fathom how much effort Tara already put into making sure she had healthy, fulfilling meals while she was staying there.

Sebastian poured Marin a glass of green juice, then offered some to CJ, who waved him off and took a sip of his black coffee.

"Do you two have breakfast here every morning?" Marin asked Harmony and Sebastian as she took a sip of the juice, which tasted unexpectedly like grapefruit. Harmony almost choked on her coffee.

"Good grief, no. Sebastian usually has to be at the restaurant first thing in the morning, but his assistant manager covered for him since he went over so late last night. I sell my dresses out of a shop downtown. It's only a few blocks from our house, so I usually just walk. We have a family breakfast once a month and this month we planned it around your arrival."

Marin felt her cheeks turn red. "That's really very sweet, but you didn't have to come here for me! Thank..." Tara cleared her throat, and she remembered she wasn't allowed to say, 'thank you,' anymore. "Right. What sort of dresses do you sell?"

"I design bespoke wedding dresses, bridesmaid gowns, formal wear... whatever someone needs!"

Sebastian put his arm around Harmony. "People come from all over to have their dresses made by Mony. She's incredible."

"I would love to see them!" Marin said before she took a bite of the pancake in front of her. Everything, from the fluffy pancake to the fresh-from-the-tap maple syrup, was delicious. Her eyes almost crossed.

CJ put down his coffee and yawned, then rubbed his eyes like a little boy who just woke up. Marin felt her heart flutter a little as she watched him out of the corner of her eye.

"We can stop by the shop while we're out and about today. I thought we could go on a tour of Wintervale, if you're feeling up to it."

Marin *was* tired from all the travel and her legs were swollen from all the walking. They offered her a wheelchair in the airport when she first got there but she turned it down. She wasn't much for drawing attention to herself in crowded places, even when she was acting against her own self-interest. Emily scolded her for it all the time. She didn't want to turn down CJ's offer but Marin also wasn't sure she could do a lot of strolling around town.

"Um..."

Almost as if he could read her mind, CJ picked up his phone and furrowed his brow. "You know what? It looks like it's going to be a little warm today. Maybe we should make it a driving tour? If Mom will let us borrow Ruby..."

Marin turned to look at Tara.

"Ruby?"

Tara crossed her arms over her chest and sighed. "My husband left me his 1953 Chevy Corvette. It almost never leaves the garage, except on special occasions. I suppose Marin's safe arrival in Wintervale could be considered a special occasion. Do you feel comfortable in a convertible, Marin?"

She had to bite her lip to stop from giggling. Ashton had *three* convertibles and never let Marin ride in them even once. When she asked him why, he said he was worried she'd throw up in them, after she got sick in the car *one time* when they were sixteen... after she'd had a high dose of medication that made her queasy.

It wasn't even his car.

"I would love to ride in a convertible! I've never been in one before! If it's okay with you, that is."

Tara walked over to a little cabinet where a ton of keys were hanging and took off a keychain shaped like a ruby.

"There are only two rules: bring her back in the shape she left in, and have fun."

Marin grinned and clapped her hands when Tara threw the keys to CJ. "I'm going to get dressed!"

"Honey, your breakfast!" Tara called after her. "You need to eat!"

"I'll take some juice to go! Thank you for everything!"

She heard everyone laughing as she rushed into the bedroom to change. It was a gorgeous day and she wasn't going to miss another second of it.

Chapter Six

CJ

It had been forty-five minutes since Marin went into her room to get ready, so CJ took the keys to Ruby and backed her out of the car's dedicated garage to wait outside. He was leaning against the hood of the car, his long legs stretched out in front of him, when his cell rang. It was Carver.

"Shouldn't you be at work, scribbling all over people's bodies?"

His brother laughed at him sarcastically. "I appreciate the respect you show my profession. I really do. Have you and Marin left the house?"

CJ looked over at the window to Marin's bedroom. He could see her shadow moving behind the curtains but wasn't sure if she was even close to ready.

"Not yet. Why?"

"Sonora is coming into the shop later for a banger and she wants to meet Marin. Her appointment is at three. Do you think you two can stop by?"

CJ rolled his eyes and looked at his watch. Sonora Albright was Carver's best friend and Wintervale's only librarian. She was always at Celestial Ink in Hadleigh, adding to her ever-growing tattoo collection.

"What is she getting this time?"

He could hear Carver scarfing down what he assumed was a Pop-Tart as his brother unlocked the front door of Celestial Ink. "She wants to add a little elephant holding a balloon to her animal-themed half sleeve."

"She still has space?" CJ asked as he visualized the menagerie of creatures that lived on Sonora's upper arm. Carver chuckled.

"The elephant will wrap it up, then we have to start on her legs, I guess. It's a good thing they love her in Wintervale because the library in Hadleigh was pretty snooty to her about her appearance. She was really upset after she went there for a children's lit reading event and a bunch of the parents essentially shunned her."

CJ shook his head.

"Snobs. Sonora loves books more than anyone I've ever met. Who cares what she looks like?"

"Who cares what *who* looks like?"

CJ looked up from the rock on the ground where he'd been staring and saw Marin standing next to him. For a fraction of a second, his breath got caught in his throat. She looked gorgeous. She was wearing a flowing, black woven dress with a pale tan slip underneath. Her long wavy hair fell loosely across her shoulders and accented the softness of her skin. Marin had on black cat's eye sunglasses, high top Chuck Taylor sneakers, and was carrying a massive black purse.

It took CJ a moment to catch his breath.

"Right, sorry. Carver's best friend. She wants to meet you today. Are you up for going to a tattoo shop?"

Marin smiled and bounced on her toes. "I would *love* to go! Ashton and Emily both have tattoos, but my doctor always told me it wasn't a good idea. She promised I could get one after the transplant, though!"

CJ furrowed his brow.

"Really?"

She nodded.

"Really really! I just have to wait six months."

CJ deflated. "It's a shame you'll only be here for two. You could have gotten your first tattoo from Carver. He's a great artist, and he has a really light hand."

"Aww," Carver said, startling CJ, who forgot his brother was still on speaker phone. "I think that's the first time you've ever complimented me, bro! I'm honored!"

"Oh, for the love of... We'll see you at three, Carver."

CJ hung up on his brother and dropped the phone in his back pocket. He was going to apologize for Carver acting like a dork, but Marin didn't seem to mind. In fact, she was already completely distracted by Ruby. Marin walked around the car and gently traced the lines of the frame with her finger.

"It's so beautiful!"

"Wait until you take a ride in it. Hop in, Marin. Wintervale awaits."

He watched as she slowly opened the door and then slipped into the seat with a contented sigh.

"It's incredibly comfortable. I never want to get out."

Charlie jumped over the door and into the driver's seat. Once he put his sunglasses on, he started the car and revved the engine a little to give Marin a feel for it. She already looked like she was having the best time ever.

"Okay, so, where to first, Miss Walker?"

She sighed in contentment as he turned the car around in the driveway and stopped at the end of the drive.

"I want to see mountains and trees and lakes and rivers! Show me the beauty of Vermont, Mr. Sutton."

CJ made a left out of their driveway.

"Your wish is my command."

Chapter Seven

MARIN

Marin and CJ spent the morning driving around Wintervale and Hadleigh, exploring the mountains and forests from the comfort of Tara's beautiful car. CJ asked her questions about her childhood in Cornwall, her mother, and her family as he pointed out the gorgeous scenery in Vermont. They were just pulling off of the Molly Stark Scenic Byway in the Green Mountains when she got a call from Ashton. He was still in Majorca with his family and as soon as she answered, she could hear a combination of static and a loud party in the background.

"Ashton? I can't hear you!"

Crackle... crackle... thumping music... crackle...

"Marin! Where are you? I called the house and..."

Crackle...

CJ cleared his throat as he parked the car in front of a bustling restaurant.

"Is that your fiancé? He doesn't know you're here... getting your transplant?"

Marin rolled her eyes. It wasn't all that surprising that he forgot where she was at the moment. It was actually more surprising he called her at all. She tucked the phone between her cheek and shoulder and shrugged.

"Ashton, I'm in America in a town in the mountains. I don't have a really great signal. Maybe you should call me when you're not at a party and we can actually hear one another?"

"America? Why are you in America? Marin…"

The line went dead, and she threw her phone in her bag in frustration. CJ took off his sunglasses and turned to her, his eyes filled with a concern that surprised her given they just met.

"You didn't tell the man you're going to marry that you are getting a kidney transplant?"

Marin sighed and rubbed her temples.

"No, I told him. I even asked him to come with me. But he's vacationing with his family in Spain and his mother refused to let him leave. She's not my biggest fan. I don't think he forgot, exactly. I suspect he's been drinking all day with his sisters and kind of…"

"Forgot."

Marin laughed sadly.

"Okay, yes. He's not a bad guy, I promise. Ashton can just be a little self-involved. But his parents didn't teach him any better."

CJ was watching her like he didn't believe her, and she couldn't blame him. She'd spent most of her life apologizing for Ashton's behavior. Given everything that was happening, she didn't have the energy to do it anymore. Marin just wanted some time to herself, where she could focus on her health and finally getting better. It didn't seem like an unreasonable request, but Ashton would probably think it was.

Maybe she would let his calls go to voicemail while he was in Spain…

"Can we talk about something else?"

CJ smiled and nodded, then gestured toward the restaurant in front of them.

"How do you feel about lunch here? The Middle Road Inn is one of the most famous restaurants in Wintervale and I know the owner will tailor the food to your needs. James and I were on the football team together in high school."

Marin couldn't help but laugh. "I feel like *everyone* in this town knows each other. Have you lived here your entire life?"

"I went to college in Burlington, but otherwise, yeah. The only one who doesn't live in Wintervale is Carver. He thought moving to Hadleigh was an act of rebellion, but he lives just across the city line. You can practically walk to his house from mom's place."

As they got out of the car and walked up to The Middle Road Inn, she could understand why someone would want to stay in Wintervale forever. The small town was bustling with families and tourists wandering the sidewalks. Stores and restaurants were full of visitors, and the noise of children playing echoed from the park across the street. It was so cozy and lovely, Marin already felt right at home. Suddenly, two months didn't feel like long enough to take in all that the small Vermont town offered.

It seemed like enough to change her life, though.

"Marin? Are you okay?"

She didn't realize how long she'd been standing on the sidewalk, staring off into the distance.

"Of course! Sorry. I was just absorbed in the atmosphere. It's such a pleasant town. Thanks for bringing me on this tour."

CJ winked at her and for a moment, her heart beat faster. She had to take a deep breath to slow it down.

"No problem. Now, let's get you some lunch. I don't want you starving to death on my watch. Mom will kill me."

Marin followed CJ into The Middle Road Inn and when she stepped inside, she couldn't believe her eyes...

Chapter Eight

CJ

CJ hadn't seen The Middle Road Inn this packed in *years*. Late spring in Wintervale was always a busy tourist season, but it felt like there were double the number of people in town that were usually there. CJ had to grab Marin's hand and pull her through the crowd that gathered in the restaurant's lobby. He saw James Everley, the owner of The Middle Road Inn and his high school buddy, coming out of the kitchen. James waved as soon as they locked eyes.

"Charlie! Come back here, man!"

CJ tried not to notice how tightly Marin was holding his hand, or how natural it felt, as he led her to James. When they finally reached him, CJ could tell his friend was exhausted.

"What is going on, James? Is every other restaurant in town closed?"

James chuckled as a server rushed past him with a tray full of dirty dishes.

"Not quite. A travel magazine did a piece on vacation destinations and specifically mentioned that Belle and I owned neighboring places in Wintervale. Within a week of the magazine coming out, my reservations booked up for months and Belle's schedule completely filled."

CJ glanced over at Marin and her brow was furrowed in confusion.

"His wife owns The Flour Girl, the bakery next door. Mom is getting a cake for you from there after the surgery, but don't tell her I ruined the surprise."

James almost dropped the pitcher of water in his hand. "*You're* Marin? Oh, wow. It's so good to meet you! Everyone is talking about you."

Marin's cheeks turned bright red. "Really? How many people is everyone?"

James smiled reassuringly as he waved at someone else who walked in.

"Nothing stays quiet for long in Wintervale. Privacy isn't exactly a thing here. But I promise you, everyone just wants to be supportive. If there's anything you need while you're here, you can let anyone know."

Marin seemed to calm down and nodded. "Thanks, James."

CJ reached over to the bar and grabbed a menu for her.

"I don't want to take up space in the restaurant. Can we get a to-go order and take it to the park? Do you have time?"

James winked. "Whatever you want. All you have to do is tell me what you need and we can make it work, Marin."

Within twenty minutes, CJ and Marin were walking out of The Middle Road Inn with two bags full of food. James went all out making a meal that Marin could eat, to the point she was almost in tears. She even hugged him before they left. As they crossed the street and walked into Wintervale Park, CJ saw a few kids from his school hanging out on the swings. As soon as they noticed him, they waved and jumped up to run over to him. He cringed and turned to Marin.

"I'm sorry. These are some of my students. They're well meaning, but they have no boundaries and they're going to ask you a million questions. I apologize in advance... Hey, Mattie! Hey, Eli! How are you today?"

Elijah Ellis and Mattie Slater were a couple and seemed to spend all their spare time together, so it wasn't much of a surprise to see them at the park. CJ *was* shocked to spot Mattie's father, Ross, and Ross's girlfriend, Wren Keller, on a picnic blanket behind them. The kids looked a little annoyed, so he suspected it was a forced family outing.

When CJ looked back at Mattie, she was talking to Marin in BSL and his heart swelled.

"You learned more than the greeting we practiced at school?" he asked as he tried not to sniffle. Mattie grinned.

"I've been working on it in case you made it back to school before the end of the year. I wanted to talk to Marin."

Eli was beaming.

"She learned so much, so fast! She really wanted you to feel welcome if you came to WHS."

Marin reached over and squeezed Mattie's hand. "You're absolutely adorable. I'm so grateful you put in so much effort. Would you two like to join us for lunch? The owner of the Inn gave us all this wonderful food."

Mattie gestured behind her.

"My dad and his girlfriend are here, too. We're having a picnic. But Mr. Sutton, will you be able to bring Marin to the end-of-year party at school?"

Truthfully, CJ forgot about the party. Every year, on the Saturday after the school year ended, Wintervale High had a dance to celebrate the end of a successful academic year. With everything else going on, it totally slipped his mind. Unfortunately, the surgery was going to be the Friday before the party.

"Our surgery is the day before, Mattie. I'm sorry. But maybe you and Eli can come visit us at my mom's house when we get home and have had some time to recuperate?"

She nodded with a smile just as Ross called over to them.

"Matt! Let them eat their lunch! Hey, Charlie!"

The kids ran off and Marin turned to CJ with her eyebrow raised.

"Let me guess... high school?"

CJ laughed, then ran his hand over his head and tried to hide how awkward he suddenly felt.

"Yeah... same year, actually. He's the sheriff now. His dad was when we were kids. Ross actually lived in New York for a while though! Some of us do escape."

Marin threw out the blanket CJ grabbed from the car. "Yes, before ultimately returning. Wintervale seems to have its own siren song that calls you all back home."

He looked around at the families in the park, the shops owned by his friends, and the students from his classes walking down the sidewalks with each other. CJ was surprised that when he saw Wintervale through Marin's eyes, for the first time in a long time, he saw what all his friends did...

A town that felt like a haven, and not a cage.

"It *is* pretty great, isn't it?"

Marin grinned as she handed him a reusable plastic plate from the restaurant.

"It really is, Charlie Sutton. It really is."

Chapter Nine

MARIN

The Transplant Surgery ward at UVM Medical Center was lovely and full of caring people, but Marin spent most of her life in the hospital. First, she was there all the time with her mom. Then, when she began dealing with the symptoms of her own ARAS, she felt like she lived in the nephrology department. Now, when she got anywhere near a hospital, she could immediately detect the antiseptic scent that filled every corner. It triggered her anxiety and made it difficult to relax.

At least now, she was surrounded by a family who did everything possible to make her feel comfortable.

Marin and CJ were all prepared for their individual surgeries and in the same room, waiting to go in. While the hospital wasn't letting over one family member in at a time, because Tara and Amber worked there, they could get Harmony and Carver in too.

The whole family was tending to both of them and getting them anything they needed. There wasn't much they could have, though, when they were an hour from going to the operating room.

"I'm so thirsty," Marin said as she watched a nurse walk by the room carrying a pitcher of water. She hadn't been able to drink anything since 8am when she took her medicine, and even then, it was only a sip to get it down. Tara sat in the chair next to the bed and brushed Marin's hair away from her face.

"It will be over before you know it, sweetie. Then you can have all the ice chips you want until you feel like eating again."

Marin sighed and nodded as she shifted uncomfortably, the IV in her arm pinching her skin. It was far from the first time a nurse had hooked her up to one of them. Still, her arms were sore from all the blood work they'd done on her since they got to Burlington.

The Suttons brought her and CJ up three days early so they could be quarantined while they ran the last battery of tests. They did most of the major parts of the workup while Marin was still at home, but the hospital was cramming the last tests in so they could be sure she and CJ were healthy enough for the surgery. Once everything cleared, they were ready to go.

Now, they were just waiting for the doctors to come get them.

CJ sighed and rolled over carefully in his bed to face Marin.

"How are you doing, kiddo? Ready to get up and go for a run?"

Marin laughed and shook her head.

"I don't think I'd make it very far with this in my arm." She held up the arm that had the IV in it and the bag of liquids hanging from the machine bubbled. Tara gently took her hand and lowered it back to the bed.

"Careful. We don't want to start a geyser."

Marin settled back down into the bed just as a doctor and nurse walked into the room. Her stomach did flip-flops at the sight of them in their scrubs. The anesthesiologist and her nurse gave them a rundown of the surgery that was to come. They'd heard everything before, but part of the process was being told what was going to happen a half dozen times before they wheeled them into the operating room. And with every new medical professional who strolled into their room, Marin got a little more afraid.

Tara must have seen the fear in her eyes.

"Are you okay, honey?"

Marin took a big breath and tried not to cry.

"I really miss my mom right now."

Tara, Harmony, and Amber all took Marin in a gentle group hug and held her close.

"It will all be okay, Marin," Tara whispered in her ear. "When you come out of that surgery, you're going to start a brand new life. And it will be wonderful."

Marin glanced over at CJ and felt tears fill her eyes.

"I know I wasn't supposed to say 'thank you' again, but it wouldn't feel right to go into this without telling you what this means to me. I didn't think I would live to see thirty and you're giving me that chance, CJ. You're giving me life."

Until that moment, CJ remained fairly stoic. But for the first time since they got to Burlington, it looked like the weight of what they were about to do finally set upon him. He had to wipe away tears from his cheeks.

"Hey, no problem. Anyone would have done the same, right?"

His mother and sisters laughed, and Marin shook her head.

"CJ, no. Virtually *no one* would give an organ to a complete stranger. This is an unfathomable gift."

Harmony sat on the edge of Marin's bed and squeezed her leg.

"You're not a stranger anymore. I hope you know that."

Marin smiled just as an enormous group of orderlies and nurses came into the room. One of them stepped forward and clapped his hands together.

"Are you two ready for your ride?"

CJ snuggled down into the bed.

"As ready as we'll ever be. Let's get this show on the road!"

Marin laughed despite her nerves as they unlocked the beds

and rolled them into the hallway. Before they took the beds in opposite directions, CJ reached out and squeezed Marin's hand. The strength of his grip made her believe they were both going to come out of this...

And her life really *was* about to change.

Chapter Ten

CJ - TWO WEEKS LATER

The Sutton house had been full of people since CJ and Marin got back from the hospital a week earlier. People were stopping by with food, flowers, and books for Marin, since she loved to read. While CJ was up and around a couple of days after they got home, Marin was still struggling with the pain. So she wouldn't get lonely, he would sit with her in her room and watch TV or play video games. Their days together were quiet, except for when Tara would roll in with Marin's immunosuppressant medications and small meals. They were all tending to her like she was a wounded bird, and it seemed like Marin didn't mind.

CJ didn't mind keeping her company, either.

It was a sunny Saturday when CJ walked into Marin's room and found her sitting in one of the comfy chairs by the window.

"Hey! You're up! How are you feeling?"

She shifted in the seat, as if she was in pain, but she forced a smile.

"Sore, but I woke up with the sudden urge to get some sunlight. Do you think we could go outside?"

CJ had asked her to go out and sit on the back porch swing

since they got home, but she'd been resistant until now. He would have hugged her if he didn't think it would hurt her.

"Let's go. We can eat breakfast out there. Mom has a dozen bird feeders and they're usually a ton of birds out there in the morning. Let me help you."

Marin waved him off and stood up on her own two feet, then walked slowly behind him to the kitchen. When Tara turned and saw Marin standing there, she almost dropped the blender in her hands.

"Honey! You're up! I was just about to bring you your morning smoothie. Are you taking a walk before going back to bed?"

CJ quickly shook his head at his mother. Given all the effort they'd put into getting Marin out of her room, he didn't want her to get the idea to go back. Tara bit her lip and poured the green smoothie into a to-go cup, then handed it to CJ to take outside.

"I'll bring you something in a minute, sweetie!" Tara called after them.

After CJ helped Marin sit down on the porch swing, he noticed she was clutching her cell phone in her hand. Her fingers were turning red from her tight grip. He sat next to her and set his hand on hers.

"Are you expecting a call or..."

She shook her head and sniffled, then unlocked the phone and handed it to CJ. At first, he didn't quite understand what he was looking at. The pictures on the screen were dark, like someone took them inside of a club. It took him a minute to realize the photos were of a blonde guy on a dance floor, passionately kissing a tall, red-headed girl. He didn't understand what was going on, or why the pictures were on Marin's phone.

"What am I looking at?"

She wiped a tear from her eye and took the phone back.

"I thought when he didn't come with me, it was because his mom wouldn't let him. There was precedent for that, you know?

But then my roommate, Emily, went on a weekend trip to London with her cousin. They happened to be at the same club where he was and saw him... doing that."

Everything clicked. She was talking about her fiancé.

"You mean, that guy making out with the red-head is..."

"Ashton. Emily sent me the pictures last night after you had all gone to bed. I texted him and told him it was over. He's been trying to call me all morning, but I keep sending him to voicemail. I think part of me always knew he was doing something like this. It was obviously too much to hope I was wrong."

CJ couldn't believe what she was saying. How could someone, let alone her fiancé, betray her in such a fundamental way when she was going through *so* much? She'd flown to another country, undergone a major surgery, and completely changed her life. And all the while, this Ashton guy was cheating on her? That was unacceptable.

"Do you want me to go to London and punch him in the face for you?"

Marin laughed so hard, it made her wince with pain, but she laughed anyway.

"No, I want you to stay right here. But thank you for the kind offer. The truth is, we should have parted ways a long time ago. It was just so much easier to stay together. We didn't know anything different. Maybe this is for the best. I can heal without wondering if he remembers I'm gone. Then, when it's time to go home, I really *can* start a new life."

Whenever Marin mentioned going home, CJ got a knot in his stomach that made him squirm a little. But now wasn't the time to bring that up; he just wanted Marin to be happy.

"I have waffles! Hey... is everything okay out here?"

His mom looked a little perplexed over what kind of scene she'd walked into. But Marin was quick to ease her fears.

"Everything is fine, Tara. Or it will be, anyway."

CJ knew she was right. Everything was going to be fine.

Chapter Eleven

MARIN

"I can't believe this, Marin. Really. Do you want me to go find him and punch him again?"

Marin had been in her room for over an hour, on the phone with Emily, going over what happened in the club. They'd talked about it so much, and for so long, it got to where Marin thought her best friend was angrier at Ashton than she was.

"Emily, I don't... wait, what do you mean *again*?"

There was a soft, sheepish laugh on the other side of the line. "I was really mad, Marin. You should have seen him. He was acting like a total..."

"Don't finish that sentence. I don't need any more visuals in my head. Can we just talk about something besides Ashton for a while? I wasted eleven years of my life on him and I'd prefer not to give him another second. How are things at home?"

Emily sighed, and Marin could hear her flop down on her bed.

"It's so dull here without you. All I do is go to work and come home, watch *Peaky Blinders*, and go to sleep."

"Hey! We were watching that together. How many episodes have you gone through?"

Emily chuckled. "Mar, from the sounds of it, I may watch TV alone forever. I'm not convinced you're coming back."

Marin gasped.

"That's... what... Why would you think that?"

It was a ridiculous question. She knew *exactly* why her best friend thought that. Ever since she got to Wintervale, and especially since the surgery, she'd done nothing but talk about how amazing life was there. Except it wasn't just Vermont, and it wasn't only the excitement she felt over her chance at a new life. Whenever she was around CJ, Marin felt butterflies in her stomach. He made her laugh so much it hurt, which was something Ashton never did. But most of all, when she was around him, she felt safe.

Still, no matter how much she protested that she and CJ were just friends, Emily saw right through her.

"Marin, darling. I can hear it in your voice. You're happy. You can claim you were content here, writing about Cornwall and going to the pub with Ashton every weekend. But we both know that isn't true and you don't have to pretend for my sake."

She wanted to argue, but she didn't have the energy for a multitude of reasons.

"I *am* happy, Emily. But the Suttons are just tending to me until I'm well enough to come home. This isn't a permanent relocation. I will be back at the cottage before you know it."

"Mm-hmm," Emily said. "I'm not buying it. I'll believe it when you tell me you're on an airplane."

There was a knock on Marin's bedroom door, giving her an out of the conversation. "I have to go, Em. I'll call you later." She ended the call before her friend could argue. "Come in!"

CJ poked his head in her room with a smile.

"Am I interrupting?"

She quickly dropped her phone on the bed and shook her head.

"I'm grateful for the distraction. What's up?"

He stepped hesitantly inside and tucked his hands behind him, like a gentleman concerned he was invading her space. "Sebastian called a few minutes ago and invited us for dinner at Wren & Candle, if you're feeling up for it. Harmony will be there, too. But if you're still tired, we can just order in or something."

Marin hadn't left the house for more than a follow-up doctor's appointment since the surgeries. She was getting a case of cabin fever, even though the cabin in question was gorgeous.

"I *am* a little tired, but I think it would be nice to go out. Are you sure you don't mind?"

CJ shrugged. "I'm sore, but Sebastian said we can have the booth in the back. They're really comfortable. Can you be ready in fifteen minutes?"

Marin glanced over at her clothes, most of which were still in piles in her suitcase. She had worn nothing but comfy pajamas since they got home from the hospital.

"Would twenty minutes be okay?"

CJ winked. "We'll make it work."

Marin tried to ignore the flutter in her stomach as he shut the door. There wasn't any time for that now. She had to get dressed for dinner at a fancy restaurant.

Chapter Twelve

CJ

W ren & Candle was as bright and beautiful as ever, and filled with the gentle hum of a dozen dinner conversations. Sebastian saved the corner booth for them, as promised. When CJ and Marin arrived, there was already a pitcher of fresh raspberry lemonade and a tray of bruschetta, waiting for them.

Marin looked like she was in awe; her cheeks were even pink from the excitement. As soon as Harmony saw them walk in, she jumped to her feet and rushed over to them.

"I'm so glad you came! Mom said you both have been cooped up since the surgery. It's great to see you out and about. How are you feeling?"

CJ helped Marin into the booth, though she didn't slide far. He could tell she was in pain after the walk from the car and didn't want to push her too far on her first night out. As soon as she was behind a place setting, Marin took a sip of the lemonade and sighed.

"I still don't feel great, but I'm making progress. It's amazing that I get to wake up every day without the fear that today is going to be the day my kidneys finally give out. I haven't known that feeling since I was a kid, and it's all thanks to your brother," she said as she gave CJ a gentle shove with her shoulder. He smiled as he handed her a menu.

"It's the least I could do."

Marin and Harmony both laughed. His sister reached over and squeezed his hand.

"Only *you* would think giving someone one of your organs is the least you can do, Charlie."

Sebastian walked up to the table carrying a tray covered in an array of appetizer specials.

"Beet salad with pistachios and goat cheese, stuffed squash blossoms, and zucchini cakes with jalapeño and lime! All low on salt for you, Marin. If there is anything else you need for now, just flag me down. Otherwise, I'll be back for your order in ten!"

He rushed off again before they could say anything. CJ loved coming to Wren & Candle, but they never saw Sebastian there if he was working. Ever since he took over the Wintervale location as manager, he never stopped moving. Marin and Harmony didn't seem to notice, though, since they were already digging into the appetizers. A squash blossom had hardly hit Marin's plate before she was slicing it in half and taking a gratified bite.

"Oh my gosh," she said between mouthfuls. "Can we eat here every night, please?"

Harmony chuckled as she scooped up another spoon of beet salad.

"I had to ask Sebastian to stop bringing food home because I was putting on Wren & Candle pounds. I swear, there was a cake in our house every night and I couldn't stop myself!"

CJ watched as Marin and his sister talked and laughed, and he couldn't help but notice how relaxed Marin seemed. She looked so content, and he *felt* so content. He never wanted anything to change.

"Charlie? What are you staring at?"

His sister's voice startled him from his daydream and brought him back to the present, where Harmony and Marin were both watching him and grinning. He didn't know how long he'd been focused on Marin's face, but it was long enough to make her blush.

"I'm sorry. I guess I was just lost in thought... Do we know what we're ordering yet?"

As if summoned by the mention of ordering, Sebastian appeared next to their table. "Have you decided what you want?"

CJ realized he still hadn't looked at the menu, so he quickly scanned through the summer farm-to-table specials that Wren & Candle offered. He was just about to order the spaghetti and meatballs with fresh heirloom tomato sauce when he felt Marin hit his leg under the table.

"Do you have a question about the menu?"

When she didn't answer him, he looked up and saw that not only were Harmony and Sebastian frozen, but the whole restaurant seemed to have their eyes on them. CJ turned to Marin, and his heart almost leapt out of his chest when he realized she was having a seizure in the booth next to him. She was just about to slump down under the table, but he managed to grab her and gently lay her flat on the seat.

"Harmony! Call 911 now! Tell them a 24-year-old woman who recently had a kidney transplant is having a seizure and to get here ASAP! Sebastian, help me turn her on her side!"

CJ tried to keep an eye on his watch and time how long her seizure lasted, but everything seemed to move in slow motion. Someone ran to the house and got Harley Thatcher, who was a firefighter in Texas, and knew how to administer first aid until the ambulance arrived. The whole time, as the world moved around them, all CJ could think was...

Please, don't take her away from me. Not like this.
Not like this.

Chapter Thirteen

MARIN

Marin woke up to a small light flashing in her eyes and groggily pushed the hand that was holding it away. When her vision cleared, it shocked her to see a stranger standing over her. He looked like he was in his thirties, but had salt and pepper hair and a beard to match. His eyes were a deep shade of chocolate brown and even through his scrubs, she could see that he was broad and muscular.

The man took a step away from her and tucked the flashlight into the pocket of his shirt.

"Marin, do you know where you are?" he asked in a voice much deeper than she expected.

She looked around, and it only took a second for her to register what happened. She was obviously in an accident and emergency, and she was groggy with a wicked headache. This wasn't her first ride on the seizure merry-go-round, though it *had* been a few years since the last one.

"I'm in an A&E and it feels like I've had a seizure?"

CJ, who was sitting in a chair in the corner, leaned forward with his forehead crinkled. "A&E?"

The doctor checked Marin's vitals on the machine humming next to her.

"Accident and emergency. It's what they call their ER in England. Marin, I'm Dr. Hardesty. I was on call when you came in from the restaurant. You had a grand mal seizure when you were in Wren & Candle, but had passed by the time you got here. I've been in touch with your transplant surgeon in Burlington and she's going to monitor your vitals from there, but for now, we're all comfortable keeping you in Wintervale."

Marin had questions, but her head was throbbing, and she couldn't focus yet. Everything in the room was still a little blurry. When CJ got up from the chair and stood next to her bed, she felt a sense of calm wash over her she was deeply grateful for.

"Hold on, Sailor. Are you sure we shouldn't go back to Burlington? How do you know it's not a complication from the surgery?"

Marin sat up and looked around in confusion. "Sailor? Where is there a sailor? I think I hit my head..."

The doctor laughed and squeezed her foot through the blanket.

"You're fine, honey, I promise. My name is Sailor. CJ and I know each other. I tutored him in advanced chemistry when he was in the eighth grade."

Marin rubbed her forehead with the hand that wasn't hooked up to an IV and sighed. "The place is smaller than St. Ives."

Dr. Hardesty patted her leg reassuringly.

"You don't know the half of it. But as far as your seizure, it's a common complication after transplant surgery. We ran your bloodwork and you don't have any infections. There is a chance it may be one of your immunosuppressive drugs, so we're going to keep you in the hospital for a couple of days and change a few of them while you're in our care."

Marin groaned and covered her eyes with her arm like she used to when she got sick of being poked and prodded as a child.

"The hospital? Again? I don't wanna."

CJ laughed softly, then took her hand and kissed the top. She felt a shiver down her spine that, for a moment, she mistook as a precursor to another seizure. Then she realized she had butterflies in her stomach, too.

"It's only for two or three days, I promise. I'm going to go see if we have a bed ready for you, Marin. You two stay put for now."

Once the doctor left the room, Marin turned to CJ and tried to ignore the swirling in her head.

"Do you know *everyone* in this town?"

CJ chuckled as he took a cold washcloth out of a basin and put it on her forehead. "Not everyone. Just most everyone. Sailor was my tutor in eighth grade, but he's also a pediatrician. He worked with my mom on a bunch of cases at Hadleigh, and Amber did her internship with him before she got hired at Hadleigh Hope. Sailor is... a lot."

Marin sighed as she took the cloth off her head and handed it back.

"I don't want to know. My head is spinning enough. I'm so sorry that I scared you and ruined our wonderful dinner. Nothing like that has happened in so long, it never even occurred to me..."

"Did you just apologize to me for having a seizure? Marin, come on."

The last time she had a seizure, she was with Ashton and his family at a fancy restaurant in London. Not only had they abandoned her as soon as the ambulance was called because they were "embarrassed by her behavior," but Ashton never bothered to visit her in the hospital. It was a little disorienting to have someone by her side that seemed to *want* to be there. She was just about to thank CJ for staying with her when the curtain opened and Dr. Hardesty walked through.

"Okay, Marin, we've got you admitted. You're going to spend two nights and three days in our finest room on the Kidney

Services floor. I will come up and visit in a day or two, but Dr. Kenny will take over your case once you're transferred."

Marin nodded as Sailor and CJ said their goodbyes. The transport people that came to move her to the seventh floor told CJ he could meet them upstairs. Before they wheeled her bed away, he reached out and grabbed her hand.

"I'm right behind you, okay, Marin? Don't be afraid!"

And she wasn't. As long as CJ was by her side, she wasn't afraid anymore.

Chapter Fourteen

CJ

It was almost 2am and while Marin slept peacefully in the dimly lit hospital room, all CJ could do was stare at her, like she was a bomb about to explode. When she had her seizure, some of the staples she still had from her surgery incision came out. Before they got her settled, a doctor stopped by to put them in again.

She was only a week from having them all removed, and now the doctor said she had to start all over again, just to be safe. Marin was upset before she fell asleep, but she was so tired, she didn't have long to dwell on it. Instead, CJ stayed awake, worrying for her.

The soft beeping of Marin's heart monitor finally started to calm him down, so he thought he might rest. He set his head down on the side of her bed just as he heard soft footsteps walking up behind him.

"You know the chair stretches out into a bed, right?"

Amber sat down in the chair in the corner and handed him a cup of tea, which he took with a grateful sigh. She was wearing scrubs and sneakers, and still had her Hadleigh Hope hospital ID hanging around her neck.

"Did you get lost on the way to work?"

She scowled at her brother.

"For your information, butthead, I just got *out* of work. Mom called and told me what happened, so I thought I'd be a sweet sister and bring you some tea. But I can take it back if you don't want it."

CJ protected the paper cup like he was playing football again. "I appreciate it! I appreciate it. Stay away. Thank you for stopping by. You really didn't have to."

"She had a seizure, CJ. Do you really think I was just going to drive by the hospital and head home for a snack? What's the diagnosis?"

"It's a common side effect from the surgery, apparently? Her CT scans were clear and her blood work was good, all things considered. Sailor was working in the ER tonight."

Amber raised her eyebrows and tried to hide a grin. She had a crush on Sailor when she was doing her internship, but he had a bit of a reputation as a womanizer. His sister was smart enough to stay away, but CJ knew there had been moments when she almost changed her mind, especially once she wasn't his intern anymore.

"Is he still around? Maybe I should say hi."

"I'm sure Tony would *love* that."

Amber's boyfriend was a Marine stationed overseas, and they hadn't seen each other in six months.

"You know I'm kidding. But at least Marin was in excellent hands. Can she go home tomorrow?"

CJ shook his head. "She'll be here for a few days. I think I'll probably stay with her."

Amber smiled at her brother.

"You should just tell her, Charlie."

He looked up in confusion. "Tell her what?"

"How you feel, Nerdface. Tell her how you feel."

CJ shushed her and checked to make sure Marin was still asleep.

"I know you think otherwise, but you don't know everything, Amber. And even if you *were* right, it doesn't matter. She's going home in a few weeks. There is no point in telling her anything. So, let's just drop it, alright?"

Amber held her hands up defensively.

"Whatever you want. But if you don't say something soon, you're going to regret it."

His sister got up and gave him a kiss on the top of the head before she left. Once he was alone, he put up the footrest on his chair and tried to sleep, but he couldn't stop thinking about what Amber said. Maybe he *did* need to tell Marin how he felt...

Before it was too late.

Chapter Fifteen

MARIN

It was really difficult for Marin to pretend to be asleep the whole time Amber and CJ were talking, but she didn't want to embarrass him. It was even harder not to say anything over the two days that CJ stayed with her in the hospital. On the ride back to Tara's house, she almost said something to him three times. But in the end, she couldn't bring herself to tell him what she heard...

Or that she felt the same way.

"You're home!" Tara said, as CJ and Marin walked through the door. "How are you feeling, kiddo? I called over to the hospital a few times to check on you, but CJ wouldn't let me come visit."

Marin turned to CJ and raised her eyebrow. "Now, why would you do a thing like that?"

"The room was small! There wasn't enough space... aw, never mind. I'm going to take a shower. Mom, can you get Marin set up?"

"Obviously."

Tara helped Marin into her room and found her some clean pajamas to change into, since she'd been wearing scrubs at the hospital. As she stretched to get out of the top, she felt a tug where

56

the new staples were put in and winced. Tara suddenly appeared next to her with two Tylenol and a glass of water.

"How did you know I needed that?"

Tara smiled as Marin took the medication.

"I *could* say it was my instincts as a doctor, but it was more like my mom senses were tingling. I'm so sorry they had to staple you up again. How are you feeling?"

Marin slipped her flannel pants on and crawled into the big squishy bed. It was so much more comfortable than the hospital bed that she thought she might fall asleep that second.

"Tired. It's amazing how hard it is to get any rest in a hospital. CJ tried to keep the nurses out of my room at night, but people were always coming and going. I think I could sleep for a week."

Tara sat on the edge of the bed and patted Marin's leg. "Maybe just until seven?"

"Seven? Why?"

She took a quilt from the other side of the bed and threw it over Marin.

"Sebastian and Harmony felt so badly about what happened that they asked to bring over takeout from Wren & Candle tonight. Do you feel up for it?"

"After two days of nothing but hospital food? That sounds incredible."

Tara stood up and gave Marin a kiss on the top of the head. It felt like an eternity since the last time she had anyone to care for her the way her mother did...

She didn't realize how much she missed it.

AFTER A LONG NAP, Marin rolled over and looked at the clock to see it was after seven. She didn't even change out of her pajamas; she just threw on a cardigan and hurried out into the kitchen, where half the family was already gathered. They covered the table in bowls of food and trays of bread and appetizers. For the first time in days, Marin was actually hungry.

"You're awake!" Amber said as she put a piece of chicken with glazed peaches on a plate. "Do you want me to make you a plate, too?"

"Please. One of everything."

Everyone gathered around the giant table and grabbed a seat, but before Marin could sit down, CJ tucked a pillow behind her back. She whispered a thank you to him as he sat down, and when she looked back, the whole family was smiling at her. Marin felt herself blushing, so she looked down at her food to regain her composure.

Tara handed Marin a small bowl of quinoa salad. "So, Marin... did the doctor say anything about flying after this seizure?"

The doctor *had* talked to her one afternoon when CJ went to the cafeteria to get something to eat, but she hadn't mentioned anything to him. She didn't know how to tell him, or the Suttons, what they said to her.

"Actually, he did. He was in touch with the doctor in Burlington and mine back home. They said it would be better if I go back so I can pick up my post surgery regimen with my doctor there. I already talked to my best friend, and she's going to meet me at the airport, then take me straight to the doctor for a checkup."

CJ choked on his tea.

"You're leaving?"

Marin nodded.

"I have a ticket for Friday."

"Three days?!" CJ said as he coughed. "You can't leave in three days."

Tara reached out and squeezed CJ's hand.

"I guess we'll just have to make the most of them, won't we, everyone?"

Everyone went back to eating and casual chit-chat about their days, but Marin couldn't help but notice how CJ was watching her silently. It didn't seem like he wanted her to leave, and if she was being honest with herself...

She wasn't sure she wanted to leave either. She just didn't know how to say the words.

Chapter Sixteen

CJ

It was Marin's last day in Wintervale, and while Tara encouraged CJ to take her out alone, he insisted it be a family day. He was afraid if he was alone with her, he would say something silly, something that he couldn't take back. The last thing he wanted was for Marin to go back to Cornwall and never talk to him. At least if he kept his feelings to himself, they could part on good terms...

Especially if she didn't feel the same way he did.

Since it was a Thursday, the usual weekend events that the town held in the summer weren't happening. That meant it was up to Tara to come up with something to do, since she was the Sutton social secretary. With Marin's permission, they went to The Skate Escape, Reid Burnett's ice skating rink on the other side of town. Reid and his wife Claudia were living in New York while she worked on Broadway, so the place felt a little empty when they walked in. Still, Sid, the assistant manager, was doing a marvelous job of keeping the place up in their absence.

As Amber, Harmony, Carver, and Tara got their skates, CJ hung back with Marin, who was headed to the snack bar for a drink. She was ordering when he sidled up next to her.

"Are you sure you can't skate?"

She turned and looked at him like he was crazy. "CJ, I had a kidney transplant three weeks ago, and a seizure three days ago. I shouldn't skate. I'm not even sure *you* should skate."

He laughed awkwardly and gestured at Sid for a cherry slush.

"I mean, if you want company, maybe I won't. But if you want to be alone or something..."

Marin rolled her eyes and gestured for CJ to follow her over to the chairs where hockey parents could wait for their kids while they practiced. They watched as the other Suttons hit the rink and started goofing around. It took all of five seconds for Carver to slip and fall flat on his butt, which made Marin burst out in laughter. She quickly covered her mouth and yelled over to the rink.

"Sorry!"

"You're fine, it was hilarious," Harmony answered back.

CJ shook his head and took a sip of his slush.

"My family is a mess. I'm the one who should be sorry."

Marin looked sad for a second, then smiled in a melancholy way that made CJ's heart ache.

"Your family is amazing, Charlie. You're really lucky to have them. And I'm so grateful to have been a part of it. It really meant the world to me."

CJ felt like there was a knot forming in his throat and he had to swallow a few times to force it back down. It was like she was already saying goodbye to him and he wasn't sure he could handle it. Instead of facing what he was feeling, he stood up and rocked on his feet for a second.

"I think I'm going to get a pretzel. Do you want something else?"

She raised her eyebrow, but shook her head. "I'm okay, thank you."

He wandered over to the snack bar again, where Sid was still standing, wiping down the counter.

"Back already, Junior?"

CJ sighed and waved at the menu.

"Pretzel with light salt, please."

Sid shrugged and went about his work, leaving CJ to rest his head against the snack bar counter. After a few minutes, he got his pretzel and went to join Marin again, but she wasn't in the chairs. In the distance, he could hear her talking to someone, but when CJ glanced out on the ice, his whole family was still there. With the quietest steps he could muster, he followed the sound of Marin's voice to the lobby of the skating rink. He inched as close as he could without alerting her that he was there.

Once he was right near the lobby door, he could finally make out what she was saying.

"Yes, Ashton. Of course, I forgive you. Why in the world wouldn't I?"

CJ felt like he was going to be sick. He'd only been gone long enough to get a pretzel? What possibly could have changed in five minutes?

Chapter Seventeen

MARIN

Right after CJ left for the snack bar again, Marin's phone rang. She figured it was Emily calling to confirm the details of her flight for the next day, so she didn't even take her eyes off the Skating Suttons when she answered.

"Hey, girl. What's happening?"

"Girl? That's something you've never called me before."

Her stomach practically dropped to her feet when she heard Ashton's voice. They hadn't actually spoken since before Emily sent the pictures of him in the club with that girl. Marin broke up with him over text because she couldn't even stand the thought of talking to him again.

"What do you want, Ashton? I'm busy."

"What do I want? I want to talk to you, Mar. Don't you think you at least owe me the courtesy of a conversation?"

Marin felt a deep, burning rage start in her stomach, then travel up her chest and into her face.

"Are you joking? I owe you..." She huffed in frustration and left for the lobby so no one could hear her yell. "Owe you? I don't owe you anything, Ashton. After years of putting up with your elitist family, your flakiness, your inconsistency, you think I owe *you* something? Come on, Ashton. Please, tell me you're not that entitled."

There was a long pause on Ashton's end, probably because she'd never talked to him like that before. The only reason they never fought was because Marin thought it was easier not to. But now that they weren't together, her dignity felt worth fighting for.

"Well? Do you have anything to say for yourself, Ashton?"

He sighed and whined the same way he did when he didn't get his way at home. "Marin, I'm sorry! It was one stupid mistake. Why can't you forgive me?"

Marin laughed incredulously.

"Yes, Ashton. Of course, I forgive you. Why in the world wouldn't I?"

"You're being sarcastic, aren't you? You were never sarcastic before. Is this something you've picked up in America from your new American friends?"

Her first instinct was to throw her phone against the wall, but she knew better than to let Ashton's snide comments get in her head. If she'd done that, she would have spent her entire paycheck on new phones over the course of their relationship. Instead, she took a few slow, deep breaths before she answered him.

"The Suttons are more than my friends, Ashton. They've become like my family. They took care of me and looked after me. They sat by my bedside while I was sick. In less than a month, they have been more of a family to me than you or your parents ever were. So, no, Ashton. I'm not going to let you off the hook. I forgive you because I don't have time to hold on to anger, but this is the last time we're ever going to speak. Goodbye."

Marin disconnected the call before he could answer her, then turned off her phone. The last thing she wanted was for him to call her back. With a frustrated sigh, she brushed her hair out of her face and returned to the comfortingly chilly ice rink. She looked around for CJ when she got to the chairs, but after a minute, realized he was on the ice with his family. Marin waved at them and everyone waved back at her but CJ, who was skating in circles like he was trying to break a speed record. She tried to get his attention, but he didn't seem to look at anything but the ice.

What could have happened while she was gone to make him so angry?

Chapter Eighteen

CJ

It had been an hour since Tara left with Marin for the airport in Burlington and CJ was still sitting on the couch in the living room, staring out the window at the light rain falling. He knew he had been kind of a jerk since the day before at the ice rink, but after hearing that she was getting back together with Ashton, he couldn't bring himself to be around her.

CJ never had a broken heart before, but he had a sneaking suspicion this was what one felt like.

When he told Marin he couldn't go to the airport with them, her sparkling, sweet eyes filled with tears. Still, she smiled bravely and told him it was okay... but he knew it wasn't okay. He was a coward, and he felt like crap about it.

"It doesn't matter how long you stare out that window, Charlie. She's not going to reappear."

Amber plopped down on the couch next to him and handed him a raspberry chocolate chip cookie she made the day before.

"I know that, Amber. I guess I just don't know what else to do with myself."

She took a bite of her own cookie and shrugged her shoulders.

"Maybe you can go back in time and make completely

66

different decisions? What is your problem, anyway? You've been totally off since the skating rink yesterday."

CJ sighed and rested his head against the cushion on the back of the sofa. He was so tired of pretending everything was normal, that he hadn't been in love with Marin since the first moment he saw her at the baggage claim when she got to Vermont. He never believed in love at first sight before, but the second they locked eyes, he knew she was the girl he'd been waiting for all his life. Like a fool, he'd just let her leave without telling her the truth about how he felt.

"I overheard Marin on the phone. She's getting back together with her fiancé."

Amber laughed so hard she choked on her cookie. "What the heck are you talking about, CJ?"

"I was looking for her at the rink and she was talking to that Ashton guy. It sounded like they were getting back together."

His sister shook her head like she was disappointed in him.

"For somebody so smart, you can be really silly sometimes, you know that?"

CJ looked back from the window. "What do you mean?"

"I mean, I talked to Marin after you went to bed last night. Her ex called and tried to get her back, and she told him to kick rocks. You obviously only heard part of the conversation."

He felt his heart drop. How could he have misunderstood her like that? She didn't *sound* like she was being sarcastic.

"Oh, God. But it sounded like... she said... and I let her go. I just let her go. Amber, what do I do? She's going to be on a plane in, like, three hours!"

Amber looked at her phone, which was sitting in her lap.

"Well, if you leave now, you can be in Burlington in an hour. You still have a chance to tell her how you feel."

CJ jumped up and ran to the hallway to grab his sweatshirt, wallet, and keys, then ran to the door. Before he could leave, though, he spun back around and stuck his head into the living room.

"What if she doesn't feel the same way? What if I blew it?"

Amber rolled her eyes. "You're never going to know if you don't at least talk to her! Hurry up and get out of here, CJ!"

He nodded his head and took off for his car. He *wasn't* sure if Marin was going to return his feelings, but he wasn't going to let her go back to England without finding out for sure...

Now, he just had to make it to Burlington before she left for good.

Chapter Nineteen

MARIN

Marin's departure from Vermont was significantly different from her arrival. Since she was leaving in the morning, almost everyone was already at work, so only Tara could take her. Amber's shift at the hospital started at noon and CJ claimed he had a headache, though Marin thought something else was going on. Their goodbye was awkward, and even though she hoped he would ask her to stay, all he did was give her a hug and tell her to write him an email.

Tara tried to apologize in the car, but Marin didn't have the energy to talk about it. She was just trying to get used to the idea of being away from a family that came to mean so much to her, regardless of what CJ did or didn't say. The separation from the Suttons was going to be hard enough to deal with once she got home; she couldn't handle thinking about the separation from CJ.

When they got to the airport, TSA let Tara help Marin to her gate, mostly because she flashed her Hadleigh Hope ID badge and they didn't question it. But she was grateful for the company and to have a friend pushing her wheelchair. Tara parked Marin by the counter and sat in the chair next to her.

"Well, honey, I'm not going to lie. I don't want you to get on that plane."

Marin's eyes filled with tears that she tried to wipe away before anyone saw, but she did a poor job.

"I don't really want to get on the plane, but I can't stay here forever, either. I've only got ninety days on my ESTA."

Tara took her hand and squeezed it. "You were only here for twenty-six. That means you can come back again, right?"

She sniffled as she thought about the way CJ walked away from her before she left their house. She wasn't sure she could come back to Wintervale just for CJ to blow her off.

"Maybe. Tara, I don't know. I thought something was happening with CJ, something special, and then... ugh! I don't know what's wrong with me," she said, and then laughed sadly.

"I know, baby. He saved your life and then he broke your heart. Charlie is a good man, but he's spent his whole life doing for others: his students, his family, his friends. I think, for the first time, he saw a future for himself with you, and it scared the heck out of him. Maybe he just needs a little more time, you know?"

Marin nodded and wiped away more tears. If time was what he needed, time was what she would give him. The only reason she had anymore time was because of CJ, so it felt like the least she could do for him. She was still trying to get her thoughts together when Tara squeezed her hand again.

"I think it's time for me to go, Marin. Are you going to be okay waiting alone for the plane?"

"She doesn't have to wait alone."

Marin and Tara turned around to see CJ standing there, out of breath, holding a plane ticket in his hand.

"How did you get back here?" Tara asked in shock.

"I bought the cheapest ticket they had going anywhere. It's a one-way ticket to New York. Since I didn't have any bags with me, they looked at me like I was going to start trouble. But I needed to talk to you, Marin."

Tara stood up and backed away slowly. "I'm going to let you two talk. I think I saw a Starbucks back there. Marin, honey, you call me anytime you want, you hear?"

She gave Marin an enormous hug and a kiss on the cheek, then punched CJ on the shoulder before disappearing into the crowded airport. For a minute, all Marin could do was stare at the man standing in front of her. He was so tall and strong and handsome, yet he appeared so vulnerable. Her heart seemed to skip beats over and over.

CJ sat down in the seat that Tara had just left and put his shaking hands on Marin's knees.

"First off, I have to apologize for the way I treated you at the house..."

"CJ, it's..."

"No, it's not fine. I was being ridiculous. I overheard you on the phone and I thought you were getting back together with Ashton, and I just freaked out."

Marin laughed in absolute shock. "You thought what?"

"I heard you say you forgave him and it sounded like you were serious."

She rolled her eyes.

"Good grief, CJ. Haven't you ever heard sarcasm before?"

He smiled and squeezed her knee. "You're fantastic at it."

"Apparently."

CJ sighed and nodded.

"I should have talked to you, but I'm not used to any of this. I don't handle emotions well when it comes to my own, and I guess I just wanted to say... maybe don't go?"

Marin looked over at the departure board for her flight. They were going to want to wheel her to her seat any minute, and she had to decide. A decision that was going to change the rest of her life.

"CJ, I think..."

A flight attendant appeared next to Marin and leaned over.

"Miss Walker? Are you ready to get on the plane?"

CJ took hold of her hand. "Marin?"

Marin looked back and forth between CJ and the door to the plane.

"I... I..."

Epilogue

CJ - THANKSGIVING

The Suttons' house was full of family, and not just the usual chaos of their family of five. Aunts, uncles, and cousins from all over the country had descended on Wintervale for Thanksgiving because Tara promised them it would be one worth celebrating. CJ was in his room, adjusting his tie, when there was a knock on the door. Carver opened the door and poked his head in the bedroom.

"Are you about ready, dude? Mom is holding the turkey for you."

CJ sighed and put on his suit jacket. "As ready as I'll ever be. What's going on downstairs?"

"The usual. The aunts are in the kitchen with mom, fussing over the food. The little cousins are outside making a snowman. Everyone is trying not to spill the secret."

"I can't believe Amber has managed to keep quiet *this* long."

Their baby sister was a notorious blabbermouth. She couldn't be trusted with anything, not even advanced notice of birthday or Christmas presents. CJ knew he couldn't stay upstairs much longer.

"Let's not keep anyone waiting."

CJ and Carver ran down the stairs so Carver could start gathering everyone in the living room. CJ made a beeline straight for the dining room, where Marin was sitting with two of his older cousins, talking about her hometown.

"Hey, ladies. Can I interrupt for a second?"

Marin locked eyes with him and smiled so brightly it lit him up inside. She looked beautiful in a dark green boat neck dress that made her eyes sparkle. Every time he walked around a corner and saw her in his mom's house, his breath still caught in his chest. He couldn't believe how lucky he was.

His cousin, Marina, popped a crab puff in her mouth and shook her head.

"This girl is a keeper, Charlie. How long are you staying this time, Marin?"

She reached out and took CJ's hand. "I decided to max out the rest of the days on my visa and stay into the new year. We'll see what happens after that."

"Actually... I wanted to talk to you about that. Marin, can you join me in the living room for a second?"

Marin looked at him with her eyebrow raised in suspicion, but nodded and followed him across the hall, where most of his family was already waiting. She looked around and laughed in shock.

"What's going on, CJ?"

Before she even had a chance to turn around, CJ got down on one knee and took his great-grandmother's engagement ring out of his pocket. It was square-shaped, with a diamond in the center and emeralds around the diamond, all set in platinum. His great-grandfather was a jeweler and designed the ring himself with stones he gathered over years of work. Tara always promised him that when he found the right girl, he could have the ring.

The moment he saw Marin, he knew it was meant for her.

When she finally circled back to him and saw him on his knee, holding the ring up to her, she threw her hands in front of her face in surprise.

"CJ! What are you doing?"

He took a deep breath and tried to put the sounds of his relatives sniffling out of his head.

"When I agreed to be an organ donor, it never occurred to me that there was a chance I'd be saving the love of my life. But that's what happened, Marin. From the first moment I saw you, I knew I loved you. Over the months we've been apart, talking and texting every day, I've only fallen in love with you more. Will you do me the honor of letting me be your husband?"

Marin leaned over and put her hands on CJ's face, then kissed him softly. When she pulled away, she rested her forehead against his.

"Looks like your kidney is staying with you after all. I will absolutely marry you."

With tears in her eyes, she signed, "I love you" to him, which he answered back the same way. He took her hand and slipped the ring on her finger, then gently picked her up and spun her around to the cheers of his entire family. When he set her back on the floor, his Uncle Frank called out to them.

"So, Marin! Are you moving to America?"

Marin laughed and nuzzled into CJ's shoulder. "I don't think Emily will be happy about me leaving St. Ives, but it looks like I'll be applying for a new visa soon."

Everyone in the family started to badger Marin about what her plans were, and CJ would rescue her in a minute. But for the moment, all he could do was look at his beautiful girlfriend, his fiancé, and think about the journey that brought them to this moment. The chances really were one in a million...

And he couldn't be more happy that he'd donated blood all those years ago.

Ingredients:

- 4 cups of cubed watermelon
- ¾ of a red bell pepper, roughly chopped
- 1 medium tomato
- ¼ red onion, roughly chopped
- 1 English cucumber, chopped
- 1 jalapeño
- 2 garlic cloves
- ½ cup Italian parsley

- ½ tsp cumin
- 4 tbsp sherry vinegar
- 3 tbsp olive oil
- 1 tsp salt, plus more to taste

Possible Garnish Ingredients:
- Finely chopped cucumber
- Finely chopped red onion
- Sliced avocado
- Clover sprouts
- Halved cherry tomatoes
- Drizzle of olive oil

Directions:

1. In a blender or food processor, add red bell pepper, red onion, cucumber, garlic, tomato, jalapeño, and 2 cups of watermelon.

2. Blend.

3. Add spices, herbs, salt, and vinegar.

4. Blend.

5. Add the rest of the watermelon and pulse slowly.

6. Add salt to taste.

7. Chill until VERY cold.

8. Serve with any or all of the garnishes! Pairs well with a dry white wine (sauvignon blanc, especially) on a hot day!

About the Author

Author photo by Crissha Figarella

Melodie March is a dreamer and a lover of nature who grew up in Vermont and can't imagine living anywhere else. When she isn't writing, she is drinking tea on her porch or volunteering at her local animal shelter. She could never pick a favorite holiday, but every winter, she's the first to start decorating her old farmhouse. She lives in Vermont on her very own Pine Street with her husband and rescue yellow labs, Honey and Lemon. If you'd like to contact Melodie to ask about your favorite Wintervale Promises character, tell her your best Christmas story, or just have a question, join her on Facebook!